Charity Fish

Kaye Giuliani

Copyright © 2012 Kaye Giuliani

All rights reserved.

ISBN: 978-1475158755

DEDICATION

This book is dedicated to my friends Kathy Parr and Kacy Thompson. They read each successive chapter with relish, and continued to beg for more. I couldn't have finished this daunting project without their unflagging encouragement, creative suggestions and support.

CONTENTS

ACKNOWLEDGMENTS i
1. THE MONSTER 1
2. GIRLS' NIGHT OUT 5
3. THE BROWN UMBRELLA 13
4. WHAT HAPPENS NOW? 19
5. TRUE FRIENDS JUST KNOW 26
6. A PEBBLE SPEAKS 32
7. LIGHTS OUT 37
8. IN PROFILE 42
9. FOR BETTER OR WORSE 48
10. WHAT'S FOR DINNER? 53
11. DEAD OR ALIVE 59
12. OUR GUY 64
13. PONYTAILS 68
14. HUNG JURY 73
15. FREEDOM FROM SPEECHES 81
16. THE FACE OF EVIL 85
17. DONUTS 89
18. RUNNING ON EMPTY 95
19. LIGHTS, CAMERA, ACTION 100
20. LOST AND FOUND 106
21. OH! *THAT* LIGHT! 112

ACKNOWLEDGMENTS

I want to thank my mother for instilling the values of love and light into every aspect of my childhood; my father for keeping copies of every word I've ever written; and my husband and children for believing in me.

1. THE MONSTER

There were no words, at first. That was the horrifying part. Before she took her first ragged breath, there was only the stinging of her abraded face, and the realization that what she had just spit out was a tooth. A knee dug into the center of her back as He bound her with one of those zip ties her Dad used to keep the tent poles together between camping trips. It was cinched so tightly that her hands became numb almost immediately.

Images of her father, tall, strong and capable flooded her with equal amounts of yearning and hope. "I want my Daddy!" she thought, despairingly, as her coppery blood mixed with tears, rain and mud in a puddle around her face. He could be on his way to find her right now. Wouldn't they be wondering why she was so late? Had mom even checked her phone messages? Charity tried to remember what she had said and couldn't. Did she mention the time at all? Would mom look to check the time the call came through? Did she even know how to do that?

Maybe this Monster would drop her and run when he heard Dad calling her name from the trail? Then Daddy could take her home and they would call the police, and . . .

Charity knew she should be pleading now. Why couldn't she do that? Beg for her life?

"Because it would be too much like yelling at the T.V.," she thought, calmer now than she would ever have thought possible. He was unthinking and unfeeling. It was obvious that she was the first step in a process of steps that he had taken before.

He stood up and yanked Charity to her feet by her elbows. Her shoulders popped and protested as they were made to bear her weight. Now the Thing had one arm around her shoulder and a knife to her throat. His breath was a rhythmic fog of stale beer and corruption as he bull-dozed her off the path and deeper into the woods. One stumble, two. There were new cuts on her throat to remind her of each. Still, not a word had been spoken, and all the while the rain continued to assault her with a cold and ruthless finality.

The umbrella would be found, maybe her tooth. She wondered if they would ever find her body. With each step the rain was working to erase any signs of their passage. Charity's foot caught in some thorny vines and she fell to one knee. The knife at her throat had cut deeply as a result and fresh blood splashed dark rubies on the leaves around her. A slant of moonlight displayed them as they turned pink and slid away in rivulets. Time was slowing. Everything had taken on an "unreal" quality.

"You're gonna' freeze in those wet clothes aren't ya', little girl? We're gonna' have to get you out of those and warm you up a bit." This was said with a smile she couldn't see and spoken into her left ear. His breath was a warm twist of sweet and sour decay. "I was worried about ya'. Out here, all alone-like, dripping wet. I like's 'em wet. . . Yes, I do."

I'm going to be raped. He's going to hurt me. I can handle this. It's only sex. Maybe he'll let me go, after? Charity knew what would happen "after." This guy radiated the kind of confidence that said this wasn't his first, second, or even third rodeo. He would take what he wanted and dispose of the evidence.

"I haven't seen your face. I couldn't identify you. If you let me go, now. . ."

His laughter was like a hacksaw biting wood. "Well, of course I'm gonna' let you go! Free as a bug from a jar. I'm just tryin' to help is all. Tryin' to save the 'lady in distress.' Why, I'm your own special prince, come to sweep you off your feet."

He had kicked her feet out from under her, then, and planted her face firmly in the forest floor before pulling down her pants. She had heard that sodomy didn't hurt if you took a deep breath first. This is one of the world's great untruths. She was surrounded by the smell of dirt and rotting things; the smells of a grave. The pain when he forced himself into her was excruciating. Screams were ripped from her that left her throat raw, but Charity's cries of anguish were swallowed by the storm.

He grunted and began to punch her, hard, between her shoulders and into her side. Each impact drove her face deeper into the mud. Though she never knew it, she was being stabbed with every thrust of his hips.

When the end came, it had been welcome. One hand had come around to grasp her forehead from behind while the one bearing the knife had flashed swiftly and deeply across her throat. Charity choked those last breaths through massive gouts of blood. Each hot surge had served to carry her farther from that merciless place.

The comforting darkness had been like being welcomed in out of the rain and wrapped in warm blankets. Her lips had formed the word "Mama," and her young life had ended.

2. GIRLS' NIGHT OUT

The knocker was odd. Charity liked odd things, so she smiled before using it. When the door opened, Janice was there. Charity smiled again. Janice was more "there" than most people because she was over six feet tall and weighed more than your average Buick. Her face was on fire with acne sores and her recent attempt to "go blonde" had failed miserably, leaving her hair a startling shade of orange. These attributes had made high school right next to unbearable for her. The magic of Janice, though, was in her smile. She smiled with her whole body, and this made her lovely. She was Charity's best friend, and had been since kindergarten.

"Heyo! I thought you'd never get here! What happened? The brownies are cold."

"That's okay." Charity answered as she pulled off her coat and joined Janice in the kitchen.

"They are chewier that way."

Janice busied herself pouring two tall, cold glasses of milk while Charity divided the entire pan of brownies onto two dinner plates.

"Billy was late getting back from soccer practice, so . . ."

"Hurry! You missed the recap from last week, but the episode is coming on now!" Milk sloshed, unnoticed, as Janice lumbered gracelessly to the family room sofa. Charity grabbed the plates and followed. The T.V. was already on and the surround sound was blasting as the girls settled into their favorite spots.

"Did you hear that Sookie and Bill are going to get married – in real life, I mean?"

"Sure. Everybody's heard that. Shh! It's starting."

A little chastened by Janice's reaction to her big announcement, Charity nibbled the corner of a brownie. Whatever Janice did to make her brownies p-e-r-f-e-c-t was doomed to die with her. What she lacked in good looks and popularity she more than made up in baking awesomeness. At any rate, the sting of being told to shut up was soon lost in their chocolate-y goodness.

The family room was cozy. Everything was mismatched and well-used. There was a musty smell coming from bookcases that lined one wall leading Charity to believe that the books had gotten wet at some point. Her mother would have thrown them away and purchased new ones. "Musty" was not allowed in their home. Neither was "Dusty," "Rusty," or "Torn." Charity liked living in a beautiful house full of new things, but she felt more at home here amid the chaos. Take this chair, for instance. She snuggled her bum into the thick cushion. It was oversized and overstuffed and she hardly noticed the shredded places where Shasta had sharpened her claws.

"Where's Shasta?"

"Shhh! I don't know. Around here somewhere."

'True Blood' had become their Thursday night tradition. Janice and her mother lived alone in this two-bedroom rancher, and Janice's mom played bridge on Thursdays. It was only a short walk for Charity, though most of it was through the woods, so she always had to check in before she started home.

Bill Compton was on the screen stumbling through a graveyard in broad daylight (which isn't particularly healthy for a vampire). The girls squealed as he began to crisp.

"No! No! Go Back!! You'll die!!"

Charity feigned horror while observing her friend. She had seen the same thing happen to her father during football games. She had her own theory about this – living vicariously through others – phenomenon. She just couldn't bring herself to yell at the T.V. Besides being absurd, it elevated the box to an importance that she considered unhealthy.

Vampire Bill collapsed into a pile of gooey ashes which signaled the sponsors to sell deodorant.

"Can you believe that?! Why would he do that?! He must just love her so much. . . "

"I know! And she was already being saved by the dog-guy, anyway."

"Sam Merlotte."

"Right. Him."

It was then that Janice realized she had finished her plate of brownies during all the excitement and made for the kitchen.

"Want some Cheese Doodles?"

"No thanks."

"A Coke?"

"Nope, I've still got my milk."

Charity's eyes scanned the French doors. It was dark out there. She thought about her walk home through the woods and shuddered. Though she'd never admit it, she often ran through the last half. For some reason that part of the woods had become choked with undergrowth, and the path was narrower there: more ominous. It was the perfect place for somebody to jump out and . . .

"Jeez! Why didn't you tell me it was back on!"

The old couch complained as she vaulted back into position. Charity imagined the puff of dust that her crash landing surely inspired.

"Did I miss anything?!?"

"No. See? Sookie has just noticed Bill and . . ."

"Oh! Good! She can give him her blood again! That'll fix him right up."

"It always does." Charity mumbled under her breath.

As the 'True Blood' episode ran down and the food ran out, Charity braced herself for the trip home.

"Oh, jeez . . . It's really raining hard out there!"

And it was. When had that started? Great.

"Got an umbrella I can borrow?"

"Sure."

Janice opened the coat closet and stuff fell out. She dug around in a box and produced a serviceable umbrella.

"Here you go. And, here's your coat."

While Charity buttoned her coat up to the collar, Janice kicked vigorously at the stuff on the floor until the closet door closed over it.

"How about my house next time?" she asked, hopefully.

"Nope. That's no fun with your folks and your brother there and all. It's better if you come here."

She had a point. Even though Billy was in bed by 9:00, her parents would have control of the remote.

Charity picked up the kitchen phone and called her mom's cell. There was no answer, so she left a message.

"Mom. I'm leaving here now and I'll be home in a few. Love you."

That was odd. Her mom always answered her cell on Thursday nights. A sick feeling started up from her toes but she shook it off.

"Okay. See you in math class."

"Oh, God, you had to remind me."

CHARITY FISH

Charity launched into the driving rain and fumbled with the umbrella. In moments, the thing was inside out and she was soaked, so she folded it up and tucked it under her arm. The entrance to the trail was hard to see if you didn't know what to look for. It started just a few feet past the bus stop sign, but you had to step over a rotten log to get to it. No. Not "step," climb over. The log was so thick that you found yourself sitting as soon as you threw your first leg across. Tonight, it was wet, and the only dry part of her was now soaked through.

She remembered thinking that nobody would make fun of her for running tonight. She hugged herself and ran. When had it gotten so cold out? Her light jacket was useless against this merciless onslaught of rain and chill. To make matters worse, streams of water that had funneled through the tree canopy, trickled down the back of her neck or splashed in the part of her hair. Several times she tripped over exposed roots or partially buried rocks, but she always caught herself before going down. Everything looked creepier tonight.

Charity didn't know when she became aware of Him. Suddenly she knew that He was behind her and coming fast. Just as she poured on an extra burst of speed, she was tackled from behind. Wham! Her face slammed into the mud and sticks with such force that she wasn't able to draw a breath for what seemed like an eternity. His body was iron. As she struggled to breathe, she was already accepting her death. There would be no math class tomorrow. She grieved for her mother, and regretted not calling for the ride home that her parents would have been happy to give her. The Thing that had her was without conscience. His purpose was clear. There would be no escape.

3. THE BROWN UMBRELLA

It was getting late when Erica Fische realized that she still hadn't heard from her daughter, Charity. She checked her cell and let out an irritated groan.

"What's the matter?" Her husband turned his head in her direction, but not his eyes – which were still glued to the History Channel.

"My battery is dead. What time is it? Shouldn't Charity be home by now?"

Dan flicked the remote to bring the time up on the screen. "Almost 11:15. Sure. She's usually home around 10:00. Maybe they got to jabber-jawing like a couple of teenage girls." He smiled, but it didn't go all the way to his eyes.

Give me your cell and I'll call the Schusters. As the phone rang, an edge of panic was just beginning to creep into her voice.

"Hello? Janice? Listen, could you please put Charity on the phone?" A pause, and then:

"What? When was that?" Now Dan was pulling on his coat.

"No. She never made. . I mean, no. She isn't home." Janice's distressed response over the phone was loud enough for Dan to hear across the room.

"Her Dad's going out to look for her right now. Yes. Yes. We'll call as soon as we find her. Thanks. Yes. She could have fallen. Yes. It is a nasty night to be out. I'm sure she is, too. Thanks, Janice."

"Where is this shortcut she's always talking about, anyway?" Dan asked as he pulled on his boots.

"I don't know, exactly." Erica's voice was trembling. "I've seen her turn off just after the White house – you know – the one at the bottom of the hill a few blocks down. All the kids use it, so it shouldn't be hard to see."

"Okay. Don't worry, honey. I'll find her. She's probably turned an ankle or something." And then, as an afterthought, "Go plug in your phone so I can let you know she's alright."

He pulled the front door open and the gust of cold air carried smells and sounds of the storm that brought Erica's anxiety up another two notches. She bolted up the stairs to plug her phone in. Maybe Charity had left a message? It took four attempts to get the charger cord connected to the phone. Her hands were shaking. Waiting for it to power up again was frustrating. At first, it looked as though there had been no messages, but after a minute she heard a tone and the message icon came up. "Yes! That's my girl! Now, tell me you're okay. Please, God," she whispered.

She held her breath and listened to her daughter's voice:

"Mom, I'm leaving here now and I'll be home in a few. Love you."

She played it again.

"Mom, I'm leaving here now and I'll be home in a few. Love you."

I could have picked her up. Why didn't I call and offer to pick her up? Why didn't I check my phone at 10:00? She called, and I wasn't there for her. Did I realize it was raining this hard? She was confused when I didn't answer. I can hear it in her voice. Why didn't she try her Dad's phone? Was she wearing a coat when she left?

What time had the call come in? A frantic examination of the main message screen told her everything. Charity had started for home at 10:05 p.m. — well over an hour ago.

Erica sat on the edge of her bed like a statue. She could feel her pulse in her throat. Something bad had happened to Charity. She wanted to cry, but couldn't. The cell was glued to her hand and they were both anchored to the power outlet.

She waited.

Once, Erica even convinced herself that she heard her daughter come into the bedroom, but, when she turned to look there was nobody there. Dan could have been to Janice's house and back three times by now. There was a sick shifting inside her then that told her she was never going to see her baby again — alive.

She brought the phone to her ear and listened to the message over and over again.

The phone vibrated, causing her to jump.

"Dan? Tell me it's good news?"

"Honey, I wish I could, but. . ."

" What? Oh my God. No. Is she hurt?"

"No. I mean, I don't know yet. Honey, was Charity carrying a brown umbrella?"

"Brown? No. She didn't have one like that. Why?"

"Good. I found one lying on the path, and it looks like there may have been a struggle or something. I've called the police, just in case. Can you call Janice and ask her if she gave Charity a brown umbrella tonight?"

"You've already called the police? Are they meeting you there, or coming here? Oh, God." She paused, took a breath and put her hand to her forehead. "Dan. Something bad has happened to our baby. I just feel it. Do you feel it?"

"Try to stay optimistic, Honey. She could have met up with a friend and decided to wait out the storm. I admit this doesn't look good, but let's. . .

"Find her, Dan? Please?"

"I'll keep looking. Call Janice and then call me back right away. The police are meeting me here. I thought it was best before the evidence. . . the, um. . . rain washed . . ."

Erica's sob finished his sentence.

"Okay. You're right. I'm sure Janice is waiting to hear from us, anyway. I'll call her now."

Honey? He asked to the soft sobbing of his wife. "Everything is going to be okay. I'm sure it is."

Janice was struck silent by the news of her abandoned umbrella in the middle of the woods. "Yes." She almost whispered it, then cleared her throat and said it again, louder this time, "Yes. That is one of our umbrellas. Charity had it with her when she left here."

"Oh, God. I just know something horrible has happened to her, Janice. Something horrible may *still* be happening to her. The police have been called."

"Have you searched the path? She could have. . . um. . . "

"Fallen. Yes. I know. Her father has been calling for her up and down the path for 15 minutes. He says there are . . . signs." Erica gulped and couldn't continue.

"Signs? Tell me! What did they find?"

"I don't know, exactly. He said there were 'signs of a struggle' – and that he was hoping the police could get there before this rain washed all the . . . evidence. . . "

"I don't care how late it is. Please call me with any news? I'll never sleep until she's safe."

"That makes two of us." Erica ended the call and noticed that her hands were no longer shaking. Was her heart still beating? She couldn't tell. Everything seemed to have gone dead inside.

4. WHAT HAPPENS NOW?

She had read lots of stories and seen movies and television documentaries about people who had died and "come back." They usually floated above their dead bodies and looked down on the scene in a dispassionate manner. Some wanted desperately to jump back into their bodies and return to their lives, but most were happier to be joining the 'cosmos' and going 'towards the light.' She didn't know if the reason that she found herself suddenly at home – walking around on the carpet, like always – was due to the fact that she had survived the attack and made it home somehow, or because she had wanted it so badly at the end to be home - walking around on the carpet, just like always.

The house was beautiful now. Like a chapel or a fairy castle. Everything glowed with love and safety. She had been wrong to think that Janice's place was where she felt most comfortable. This was home. It always had been, and always would be.

When Charity found herself standing in her parent's bedroom without ever having taken the stairs or walking the length of the hallway, she knew she was dead. This knowledge was not particularly distressing for some reason. Her mother was sitting on the edge of the bed with her cell phone in her hand. They knew she was gone. At least, her mom did.

"Mama?" *Hadn't that been her first word? Now, it was her first word as a dead person. Imagine that.*

Charity didn't know whether or not she had spoken out loud or just thought the word. This was all kind of new for her – being dead and all. But, her mom turned just then and looked right at her.

"Mama? Can you hear me? I'm right here with you, Mama, and I'm okay. It was awful, but it's over now." The words were spilling out all in a rush. Charity had so much to tell her. She wanted to get a hug and maybe a mug of hot cocoa with those little marshmallows all melting on the top. . . But, her mom had turned back right away and was talking to her daddy about the police.

On second thought, maybe she didn't exactly need the cocoa – in a real way – anymore. She just needed the comfort it gave. She needed to sip it slowly and hold the warm mug in her hands. She needed to talk and talk and talk about everything that she had been through, and about what it was like to be dead.

She thought about her little brother and – whoosh! – she was standing next to his bed. 9-year-old Billy was sleeping on his side, with one leg thrown over his rumpled covers. He had on one white sock, but the other foot was bare. Billy had her Dad's fair hair, where she was dark-haired and brown-eyed like her mom. *Well, I used to be*.

Charity couldn't resist the idea of laying a hand on his shoulder and trying to shake him awake. She needed to tell Billy that she was okay before everybody started wailing and crying and the police started turning their house inside out looking for clues. *As if they would find any here, in her fairy castle. Nothing evil or corrupt had ever been allowed in her house.* She wasn't even sure she could touch him. She hadn't tried to touch anything yet. His soccer-ball lamp was on the bedside table and she reached for the button to switch it on. 'Click!' The light came on just as it always had. Billy stirred slightly, but didn't wake.

She walked around and sat down next to him on the little bed that used to be hers. Had she ever been mad at him? Had he always had such long lashes and that pale constellation of freckles across his nose and cheeks? All of her love for her brother came flowing up through her like light through a filament. When she laid her hand on him, he sat up and rubbed his eyes.

"What? Why did you wake me up?"

Can he see me? I think he can.

"Billy. Can you hear me?" she asked, with her hand still resting on his shoulder.

"'Course I can hear you. What'cha' want?"

"Billy, something has happened. But, I want you to know that – whatever they say – I'm okay now. Will you remember that? I'm not here the same way I used to be, but I'm not hurt or afraid, either. Got that?"

"What are you talking about? What do you mean you're 'not here?' Are you nutso?"

"Yes. That's it, exactly." She smiled. "I'm nutso. Now, go back to sleep and remember what I told you."

"Nutso, futso, schmutso . . . " He murmured, as he snuggled back into his covers.

"Charity?"

"Yes."

"Turn out the light, will ya'?"

"Yes, Billy. I'll turn out the light. I love you."

She switched off the light and found herself standing back out in the woods with her Dad and two policemen. They had found the umbrella. She looked and could see the tooth lying in the bottom of the puddle where her face had been. It might have been a pebble, but it wasn't. The storm had blown over, but water was still dripping from all of the leaves.

They were looking at the torn-up earth and broken branches.

"Mr. Fiscee, is it?"

"No. Fische. It is pronounced "Fish."

"Oh. Sure. Sorry." The short cop looked down at his clipboard. "Listen, Mr. Fische. Kids this age go missing for lots of reasons, but they always turn up in the end – full of apologies and excuses."

"Not Charity. She left her friend's house just after 10:00 p.m. and was headed home. That's only a short walk down this trail, a left turn, and a couple of blocks. She was walking through a storm wearing a windbreaker and tennis shoes. It is plain that something happened here. Some kind of struggle. Why would she leave this umbrella behind?"

"Still, I'm sure you understand that we can't begin a serious investigation until she has been missing for at least 24 hours. See these kids..."

Her dad stood up to his full height and moved towards the policeman. "By then any evidence will have been washed away!" At least take some photographs, look for footprints."

"You really should pick up my tooth, while you're here, too." She said to the cop. "It's sitting in the bottom of this puddle next to your foot."

The policeman got a strange look on his face and turned his head in her direction. Charity laughed. This being dead thing might be kind of fun once she got used to it.

"Well, you have a good point there, Mr. Fische. I guess it couldn't hurt to have a look around. But, we can't file an official 'Missing Persons' report until tomorrow."

Her dad slumped a bit, visibly relieved that evidence was going to be collected.

The taller cop with the coffee-and-donut belly was called over and they divvied up the search areas. The first cop turned to her dad and said, "You should go home now, Mr. Fische. You are soaked through, and I know your family is worried. We'll do what we can here, and stop over to talk with you when we're through."

"I'd rather stay and help." He said. Charity looked at her frozen, drenched Daddy, and that love-light came flowing up through her again – brighter than sunshine.

"Daddy. He's right. Go home and be with Mama. She needs you right now more than I do."

She saw his head bow slightly. Was that a tear on his face?

"On second thought," he said, "You're right. I'm needed at home."

"That's exactly right. You go on home and wait for us. We'll do our best here."

"Find her. Please."

He made sure the cop was eye-to-eye when he said it, too. Gosh, she loved her Daddy.

Charity's head came up with a start. "Janice! Oh horse poop-on-a-stick! What is this going to do to her!" *You know exactly what will happen. She is going to blame herself. Then, sure as wasps crawl into soda cans she is going to turn off that beautiful smile and bury herself under a shitload of Ding Dongs.*

She looked around for witnesses. *Can I even say "shitload?" I mean, are the profanity police going to drag me to hell by the heels?* Raisins being the better part of oatmeal, she opted to lay off the swear words from now on. It couldn't hurt to be careful.

5. TRUE FRIENDS JUST KNOW

Janice was pacing back and forth between the family room and the kitchen phone. Her mom wasn't back from the bridge club yet, and she was tempted to call over there and tell her to come home. This was bad. People could say what they wanted, but she knew Charity. Charity didn't disappear. She was solid like the moon – even when you couldn't see her, you knew right where she would be. *Dependable*. She had been on her way *home* for God's sake! They didn't *have* any other friends. She avoided smokers at all costs, had a deathly fear of anybody who used drugs, and hadn't had so much as a *crush* on a guy since 1st grade! They weren't 'teens' in the usual sense of the word. She didn't have a rebellious *anything!*

No. If Charity was missing, then someone had taken her. Janice opened the fridge and pulled out the leftover fried chicken. Still pacing, she pulled strips of white meat from the breast and chewed furiously.

A white Persian cat sprang to the countertop in pursuit of chicken. Janice was oblivious to the fact that her cat was helping itself to a drumstick, and that was just fine with Shasta. Eyes half-closed, the cat immersed herself in the whole "chicken" experience: every now and then reaching into the casserole dish to re-position the chicken leg then immediately licking her paws. Whether this was for cleanliness or tastiness would be a question for the cat.

When the phone rang, Janice lunged for it. "Hello?" She put down the chicken breast and ripped off a paper towel. "What? Yes." She cleared her throat and said it again. "Yes. That was one of our umbrellas. Charity had it with her when she left here." She gulped. *Charity*. This was bad. She pulled a chair away from the kitchen table and plopped into it.

"Have you searched the path? She could have. . . "

"What kind of 'Signs?' Tell me! What did they find?" Janice heard her mother's key sliding into the lock before the door swung open.

"I don't care how late it is. Please call me with any news? I'll never sleep until she's safe."

"Til who's safe?" Her mother dropped her purse, keys and half a bundt cake on the table and started unbuttoning her coat.

Janice turned mournful eyes towards her mother and began to grieve.

The story came out between sobs and forkfuls of leftover cinnamon bundt cake with drizzled confectioner's sugar icing. Charity slipped into a chair somewhere in the middle of the story and eyed the cake. Mrs. Schuster was a good cook. Charity had always been normal-sized, which was amazing considering her love of all things dessert. When Janice said, "She could be out there, right now, being hurt by some creep!" Charity said, "But, I'm not. I'm right here."

Neither one of them acknowledged her presence in any way. Maybe it only worked sometimes? Or, maybe Janice sensed that she was already dead and was in "denial mode." She wondered if she would become less visible / audible over time?

Then, there was Shasta. The cat looked up from her strenuous paw licking and stared Charity square in the eye. "Hi, kitty. Remember me?" Done with the chicken for now, Shasta jumped down and sidled over to Charity to be worshipped and adored. She rolled onto her back and half-purred, half-meowed an invitation to rub her belly. Charity rubbed that fuzzy belly and talked baby talk to Shasta just as she would have a few hours earlier.

Shasta took her "deadness" in stride, apparently. It was comforting. She made a mental note to get herself a cat.

The tall glasses of milk were poured, theories were bandied about, and now both mother and daughter stared at the phone.

"Will they call us again tonight?"

"I asked her mom to call us tonight."

"Even if they don't find anything?"

"I told her I would be up and worried. . ."

"Maybe we should call?" Mrs. Schuster nibbled on a freshly-manicured nail.

"No. They'll jump out of their skin every time the phone rings – thinking it's her."

"Oh. Yeah. Probably."

"Well, we can't stare at the phone all night. I've got work in the morning, and you have to be at. . . "

"No. No, mom. I can't go to school tomorrow knowing that Charity is missing. I just can't!"

"Don't you have a math exam tomorrow?"

"Yes. I do. But, Mom, . .please don't make me go to school tomorrow. I won't be able to stand being anywhere until they find her."

"You said it yourself. You won't be comfortable anywhere, so you might as well be uncomfortable at school." There was an implied "This subject is closed." At the end of that last sentence, and Janice wasn't about to jump through that ring of fire, so she sighed and resolved herself to be miserable for the foreseeable future.

"Come on, kiddo. No point in waiting by the phone." She eyed the clock on the microwave.

"It's 2:00 a.m. I doubt we'll hear anything more tonight."

"Okay. I'll be right up. I'll put this stuff in the sink to soak."

Mrs. Schuster turned halfway up the stairs and said, archly, "Why not just stick it in the dishwasher, while you're at it? Really. How much more effort does it take. . ."

"Okay! Okay, mom. No problem."

In the quiet kitchen, the water ran. A plate clanked a glass as it was placed into the dishwasher. It was in the few moments of absolute silence, just as Janice turned to climb the stairs that Charity tried again. She quietly stood up and moved to drape her arm around her best friend's shoulders.

Janice was very still. She bowed her head and – her voice barely audible – she said "Charity? If you're here. You know, like ghost-type here? I want to tell you that I love you. You were the best friend anybody could have ever had. I'm thinking you are dead. I don't know why I'm thinking that, but I am. And, I'm thinking that you would want to come and tell me that it wasn't my fault and stuff like that, because you'd do that. I know you would. And, if it sets your heart at ease, I'll promise to let that go and get on with my life – even though I should have made you call your folks for a ride – and even though I should have at least offered to walk you home – and even though". . . She began to cry, softly now. "I made you come to my house when you wanted to meet at your place."

Crying steadily now, Janice climbed the stairs to her bedroom. She'd said all she needed to say.

Charity smiled because true friends just know, and they were, and would always be the best of friends.

6. A PEBBLE SPEAKS

Officer Gentry followed his instincts and called a forensics team out to collect evidence surrounding the last known whereabouts of the missing teen. He wasn't exactly following protocol, but the father had made a good case for abduction, and he didn't want to be the one to have to follow a cold trail after the fact. When a tech came to him with the tooth, he knew that his instincts had been right on. Also collected were several shoe impressions and more than a few strands of long, brown hair. DNA analysis would come into play later, but he felt certain that all of the DNA would come back to Miss Fische.

He was excited to have something to tell the parents, but that was leveraged by the fact that this news would not be well-received. The shoe impressions were only good near the creek where they had crossed an area mostly made up of clay. Two size 7s were closely followed by the impression of a man's size 10 or 11 hiking boot.

Before leaving the scene, Officer Gentry authorized the use of a canine unit. He knew that the chances of finding this young lady alive were slim to none. It would fall to him to relay this information to her family, as well. It wasn't his favorite part of the job. At least he could assure them that everything was being done that could be.

"Ben." Gentry's partner turned at the sound of his name and walked up the hill to meet him.

"I'm going to talk with the family now. Want to come along?"

"You're on your own, Mike. I handled the last two, and Metro was a particularly messy one, if you remember." They both made a face. That had been a case of "Train meets human" and anyone will agree that's an ugly match-up.

"Okay. I'm on my way. Crap. I hate this part."

"Just take a deep breath and give them the truth without a lot of pussy-footing around. No false hopes. That kind of stuff will just jump up and bite you in the ass later."

"Right. I'll be back here in about 30 minutes. Can you brief the canine unit?"

"Will do."

He pulled into the driveway of 492 Chandler Street at 10:00 a.m. The front door opened and Mr. and Mrs. Fische were waiting for him before he could even get the squad car into park. It was clear that neither had slept. He grabbed his clipboard just so he'd have something to fiddle with and flip through when things got too emotional.

Mrs. Fische took one look at his face and turned away from the door. She already knew it was bad news. When Mr. Fische welcomed him inside, she was sitting woodenly on the living room sofa looking at her hands.

"You've found something?" Daniel Fische asked.

"We have." He paused and urged Mr. Fische to take a seat before he continued. Officer Gentry sat down across from them on a loveseat. He cleared his throat. "We now believe that you were correct in deducing that your daughter was abducted."

"Tell us. Please. It has been awful - not knowing." Dan said.

"We brought in a forensics team last night and they have found sufficient evidence to support a full-scale criminal investigation into the disappearance of your daughter." He shifted the clipboard before continuing. "We found a broken tooth very close to where the umbrella was discovered." This brought sobs from the child's mother. He forged ahead. "We also retrieved several long, brown hairs from the woods adjacent to the trail, as well as three shoe impressions; two of which were believed to have been made by your daughter, and the third belonging to a man wearing size 10 or 11 hiking boots and weighing between 250 – 275 lbs."

"She's gone, Dan. Our baby's gone. I've known since last night. We'll never. . ." The sentence trailed off into tears as the couple embraced in shared grief.

"Was there any evidence that she had been. . . that she was . . .?" Charity's father asked, unable to finish.

"No sir. While that is good news, we all need to remember the severity of the storm. Any blood evidence would have been diluted significantly by that kind of downpour. We have canine units coming to the scene, however, to see if there's anything else to be found. Please rest assured that we are doing all that can be done to find Charity."

"You don't think we're going to find her alive, do you?"

The officer sighed. A direct question required a direct answer.

"No sir. The odds are not in her favor. But, we're not giving up the search by any means. We'll make every effort to find her and bring charges against her assailant." This seemed like a good opportunity to stand up and excuse himself. "We will keep you informed as the investigation progresses, of course. If you have any questions, or can think of anyone who might want to harm your daughter, please call me." He handed Mr. Fische his card. "My home number and mobile phone are both there. You can call at any time."

The father walked him to the door and shook his hand. "Thank you, so much, for going ahead with the forensic team. It means a great deal to us."

"You're welcome, Mr. Fische. You'll hear from us as soon as we know anything."

It was a relief to climb back into his squad car and buckle up. That had been awful, but it was over. He picked up a Big Gulp® at the 7-11 before returning to the scene. The hardest work was still ahead of him. Officer Gentry needed to catch this guy before he did it again.

7. LIGHTS OUT

Charity had no desire to find the Monster. Her current feeling of safety and well-being made the horror of those last moments seem very far away and unimportant. She began to learn how to control her wild thoughts, as she would always find herself smack in the middle of whatever she was thinking about. Showing up during the third-period math exam had been decidedly unpleasant, at first. School had never been a comfortable place for Charity, and math had always been especially frustrating. She had just turned to leave when she remembered Janice.

There she is, and she doesn't look happy.

Sitting at the absolute last desk in the furthest corner of the room, sat Janice. Her pencil was not moving confidently across the page. As often happened these days, Charity found herself standing behind her best friend in a flash.

"I am here to save the d-a-y!" She sang out loud to the tune of the Mighty Mouse theme song, while placing one hand on her hip and raising the other to the sky in the classic super hero stance. Janice looked up, but nobody else reacted.

It was a simple thing, then, to move about the room and bring the answers to the absolute last desk in the furthest corner of the room. Sometimes, she had to yell them at the top of her voice and dance around before Janice's pencil would comply. Yes. It was cheating, after a fashion. But, then again, what good was it to have a dead best friend if you couldn't even get some help with your math exam?

Janice wasn't confident in her answers. She probably thought that she was pulling them from the air just so she'd look busy like everyone else. Charity grinned. Wouldn't she be surprised when the grade came back? Charity hoped she would still be around to enjoy that moment. More and more, though, she didn't think she would. She felt a pull that was getting harder and harder to ignore. The time might be coming when she would have to leave this life she loved behind and move on to whatever came next.

Though she was tempted to screw around with some of the bully types, (Cheryl Claggett, Peter Granger)

Charity hopped schools and joined her brother in the middle of his art class, instead. She was happy to see that he was laughing and talking animatedly with friends as he cut large shapes out of brightly-colored tissue paper.

"My sister's missing."

"Gee. I wish *my* sister would go missing!" The red-headed boy chirped from across the table.

"What happened to her? Did she get kill-ded or somethin'?" This from a tiny dark-haired boy; his startling blue eyes open wide.

"Yep. I think she got herself taken and kill't last night in Harlan's woods." He said with a sense of importance. "But she's okay now."

"What? How can she be okay if she's all dead?" Red challenged.

Charity grinned. Billy remembered her visit. She had gotten to him in time.

"'Cause her ghost came and woke me up and told me stuff."

"Naw! That's a lie! There's no such thing as ghosts!" This from Red again, who was getting a bit too aggressive.

"Is not a lie! Her ghost told me that she wasn't there like she used to be, but she was not hurt nor afraid no more. Then, she turned out my light and left."

"Ha! Ghosts can't turn out lights like living people! You're making this up."

Worried that this childish interaction might be headed into 'fight' territory, Charity chose that moment to flick the three switches that would leave the room in complete darkness. By the time she had turned them back on, Billy was grinning from ear-to-ear and all talk of "ghosts" had come to an abrupt halt.

"Thanks." He thought loudly.

"You're welcome." She said into his ear as she reached out to ruffle his blonde curls.

Billy moved his hand to the top of his head and ducked down with a smile.

It had been a busy morning. Charity knew she should spend more time with her mom, but it was impossible to break through the anxiety, fear and grief that had grown up like a wall around her. In a way, it was as hopeless as screaming out there in the woods on that stormy night. Every word Charity spoke was being carried away by the churning emotions that raged and swirled and barricaded her mother into that state of dark isolation.

Dr. Kurtz had prescribed sedatives, which Mama had repeatedly refused to take. Dad had even picked them up from the pharmacy for her, but they were still on the counter, primly stapled inside the white CVS bag they came home in.

If mom would just take the pills and go to sleep for a while, Charity felt sure that she would be able to calm her. All she needed was for the chaos to recede long enough for her to wrap her arms around her mother and let her know that she was okay.

Dad had been so easy to approach. He was filled with grief and sadness, but the acceptance of her death and assurances Charity had conveyed were evident in his strength. Of course, Dad had to be the strong one, didn't he? It was expected of him. Charity felt sorry for him, now. That must be hard. The one emotion that she had no control over, however, was his anger.

Daddy wanted revenge. It was consuming him. He shadowed the efforts of the police, and his face had gone all hard and mean. And, even though Charity no longer cared about the Monster that had tortured her and taken her life, she was gratified by the need her father had to catch the guy and beat the snot out of him.

It was wrong for her to feel that way. She wasn't sure why, but the wrongness rang out with the clarity of the huge, iron bell in the church tower downtown. She knew that she needed to lift the need for revenge from her father's heart, but just couldn't bring herself to do it. Not yet, anyway.

8. IN PROFILE

Weeks passed, and still there was no sign of Charity. The police had changed the status of her case from a "Missing Persons" to a "Homicide Investigation." The dogs had led the canine division through the woods and out to the highway before losing her scent. Some tire tread impressions had been found in the shoulder and molds were made to add to their growing cache of evidence.

Witnesses had observed a dark green or black Ford F-150 parked on the shoulder during the storm. Some had even considered pulling over to wait it out themselves. It wasn't until Charity's disappearance had hit the evening news that anybody had thought to report it. The tire impressions they had lifted from the scene were consistent with the Firestone Champion HRs that came standard with F-150s, so a list was pulled of every green, black, or dark blue F-150 that had been registered in the state of Virginia that year. That was a *long* list.

A profile of the assailant was created, which helped to narrow their search considerably. The man they were looking for would have these characteristics, according to the profilers:

- Male, over 6ft. in height, weighing over 325 lbs.
- Aged between 35 – 55
- Probably had an arrest record for prior sexual assaults
- May have served serious time
- Lived locally and was familiar with the area in which the crime had occurred
- May have been watching the victim for some time
- Lived alone
- Unable to relate to women
- Probably employed doing some sort of manual labor
- Very muscular

The work was grueling and still they had no suspects, no body and no murder weapon. The family was pushing for answers that nobody had. A "Tip Line" had been set up and the calls were hard to keep up with. Some callers swore that they had seen Charity in this mall or that mall, others just knew that their boyfriend / husband / neighbor had killed her and dumped the body here, there or somewhere else. All the leads were worthless. All of the searches had come up empty.

Charity was aware of the efforts being made on her behalf. As for her – she had no idea where her body might be. Unlike others she had read about, she had opted to get away from the scene and the perpetrator. When last she'd seen it, her body had been used up, torn, broken and debased. The very moment she was released from the pain and horror of that awful night, she had embraced the freedom to leave it all behind and had done just that!

Now that time had passed, she was finding it hard to remember much about that night. It didn't seem important anymore. Charity was focused on the people she loved. After all, they were suffering right now, and that was a clear priority over some half-remembered trauma she had endured while she was still alive.

In an effort to be helpful, she had concentrated very hard on trying to locate her body. Maybe it was one of those "special powers" that you got when you died? But, no amount of quiet meditation would provide a clue. She had taken it off like ruined clothing and was glad to be rid of it. End of story.

The most disturbing part of this mystery was the way in which it was impacting her mom. Mom was frantic to bury her! It was as if she would be unable to accept Charity's death until she had her body in a proper box and could lower it into some proper dirt. From Charity's new perspective, this made no sense at all. She watched as her mother paced and wrung her hands. She saw her jump whenever the phone rang, then deflate when it wasn't Charity on the other end. She was inconsolable.

Even in her sleep, her mother's defenses were up. She refused to accept what she already knew, deep down, because accepting it would mean she was never going to plan a wedding, or attend the birth of a grandchild, or any of the dozens of other events that mothers plan before their daughters are even conceived.

Charity had made every effort to comfort her – to help her understand that being dead was no big deal – to tell her that she was "A – Okay." On a couple of occasions she had even been certain that her mom had been able to see her, but denial had won out every time. Dad did his best to be a comfort, but he was consumed with the need for retribution. Billy seemed to have been left to his own devices. It was assumed that he was too young to understand the finality of death, and that he was handling things well, so why rock the boat?

Billy. He was the answer. He would have to be the one to talk to mom and dad. He would get through!

Charity waited until the house was fast asleep before manifesting in Billy's room. He had taken to sleeping with the stuffed dog she used to keep on her bed. It was a white poodle with pink bows that had been more of a decoration than an actual plaything, and it was decidedly out of place in this sports-inspired, all-boy-all-the-time room, but she was touched by his need to have something of hers nearby.

Like before, she switched on his light. But, this time, Billy was awake instantly and looking around his room for her.

"Charity? Is that you? I can't see you, Charity."

Try as she might, she couldn't make herself visible to him. Instead, she picked up the poodle and held it in her arms.

"I knew it was you! Gosh, we miss you something awful, and mom and dad are going crazy."

"Can you hear me, Billy?"

"Why don't you go and see mom and dad, too? They don't believe me when I tell 'em what you told me."

So much for having a chat.

Charity scanned the room for inspiration. There had to be a way to get through to him. Her eyes rested on the little bookcase next to his desk and chair. Excited now, she skimmed the familiar titles and exclaimed when she found the one she had been looking for. "I'm Okay, Mommy," by Sherry Toothman[1]. She had been with her mother when she bought the book after one of Billy's

---

[1] "I'm Okay Mommy," by Sherry Toothman. Publish America, 12/30/2007. ISBN-13: 9781424187331

second-grade classmates had lost his battle with Leukemia.

She brought the book over to Billy and put it in his hands.

"Oh. I remember this one! This is perfect! Okay. You want me to give this to mom and dad?"

She flicked his bedroom light off and on.

"Okay, Charity. I'll tell them you wanted me to. They won't believe me, but I'll do it."

She kissed his forehead, put the stuffed poodle under the covers with him and turned off the light.

"Goodnight, Sis. I love you."

9. FOR BETTER OR WORSE

At first, there had been an endless wave of questions. The police, then the homicide detectives, the school counselor, teachers and kids that had wanted nothing to do with Charity prior to her disappearance. "Did Charity have any enemies? Did she ever mention a guy who was hanging around, giving her the creeps? Was Charity involved with any guys? Did she have a drug problem? Alcohol? Did you ever notice a green, blue or black Ford F-150 cruising around the neighborhood, or parked where it didn't belong? Was Charity depressed? Had she ever been suicidal? Did she spend a lot of time in online chat rooms? Could Charity be pregnant? Did she ever mention running away from her parents?"

The reporters wanted to know things like: "What were her last words? Had she walked that path every

Thursday for the past few weeks? Was she afraid to walk home that night? Did you ask her to stay until the storm passed over? Did you offer to walk home with her? Did Charity get along well with her parents? How long had you two been friends? Would you say she had been a good friend to you?"

They were looking for sappy, tear-jerker hooks to pull in their audiences. One or two of these news hounds had actually seemed to care, but the rest were just doing their jobs in an extremely competitive environment and were desperate to get their hands on that touching old photo or the especially thought-provoking quote that would win them a raise or a promotion – or both.

That following spring and summer, Janice had plodded through her days on auto-pilot. She hadn't been able to watch a single episode of "True Blood" since that night. Kids had started using the path again, but still tended to move through the woods in groups. There had been all kinds of crazy rumors about werewolves and vampires stalking Harlan's Woods. Some versions had Charity eaten on the spot – bones and all – others had her transformed into a "creature of the night." That high-school juniors could come up with that kind of crap was not as surprising as the fact that some people actually *believed* it.

Janice ignored them. Whatever made girls afraid to walk through those woods alone was a good thing. Everybody knew that the shortcut was too tempting to avoid for long. It took a good eight blocks off of a trip to the mall, and at least four from their walk to school. For now, parents were driving their kids to and from work, but how long would that last? Sooner or later somebody would oversleep, be late for school or work, and be forced brave the trail alone.

Everyone was afraid right now. Doors and windows were locked. Alarm systems were suddenly big business. Janice's neighbors had adopted a German Shepherd from the SPCA that barked all night and drove everybody crazy. For the first time, she actually missed her mother on Thursday nights, and kept every light in the house on until she got back. Mrs. Fische had said that this guy might have been following Charity for some time – just watching. If so, that sick freak had been right outside – maybe more than once.

Still, though this had been a traumatic time for her, this was also Janice's first time in the spotlight. Peers were claiming her as their "friend" in order to garner a share of local sympathy or to catch a ride on the "media circus" train surrounding Charity's disappearance. Suddenly, the phone rang with invitations to "hang" at the mall, or "catch" a movie on Saturday.

Without realizing it, Janice had been undergoing a slow metamorphosis. Pounds had been falling away; blemishes clearing up. The smile that Charity had loved so much was starting to be noticed by others. As is sometimes the case, through flames of unrelenting anguish a strength of character can be forged; an empathy for the suffering of others, and a diminished obsession with one's self. She was becoming a beautiful person.

Charity watched this transformation from her favorite chair in the family room, or playing with Shasta on the floor while Janice wrestled with her homework or chatted on the phone. She remembered how Janice used to cut her off mid-sentence and had a tendency to discount everything she said. Charity had never liked that trait, but had been able to dismiss it as "Janice being Janice." Friends were supposed to overlook little character flaws, after all, and embrace each other's individuality – warts and all.

The new Janice was still and centered. She listened, and was careful with people's feelings. This inner quiet had replaced her need for food as a source of comfort. The improved eating habits had worked wonders on her troubled complexion, and the new clothes had gone a long way towards removing the walls of shabbiness that Janice had been hiding behind for years. Watching Janice bloom had been better than TV.

Would these miracles have taken place if she had survived the attack? Charity wondered, not for the first time, if her death had been part of a bigger plan. She had never been the religious type. Her family didn't attend church. Come to think of it, she had been dead for quite a while now and she'd not seen one "heavenly being."

Wasn't dying supposed to give you the answers to the big questions? Had she done something wrong? Missed the light or the bus or the chariot or whatever? Maybe she should have stayed with her body?

With her head full of big questions, Charity turned to find herself back home.

10. WHAT'S FOR DINNER?

Dinner was pizza. Again. Billy used to love pizza, but ever since Charity was murdered it had been pizza and burgers and pizza and burgers. Nobody cared if he ate his meals in front of the TV, or while he played video games. To be honest, nobody seemed to care whether or not he ate at all. His mom rarely ate these days, and when she did it was in a distracted way. She drank quarts and quarts of coffee. She had also started smoking.

His father worked a lot of overtime. When he got home it was dark out and he fell asleep on the sofa in front of the television. He would yell at the police and the newspapers and the radio station people. Billy would try to get his attention – first by excelling – then by acting out in school. When neither of those worked, he tried making jokes and being a clown. Any mention of Charity was shushed because Dad didn't want to upset Mom, or the other way around.

When Billy asked for money, they gave him money. When Billy asked if he could stay home from school, they let him stay home. He missed his sister, his parents and his family. He missed mom's famous 'Chicken-a-la-king,' home-baked pies, cakes and cookies. Home didn't smell, sound, taste or feel like home anymore.

Then Charity had come back! His light had come on in the middle of the night, and he had known it was her right away. He couldn't see her this time. He couldn't hear her, either. But, she had figured a way to let him know, for sure. She had made that toy dog float in the air! No strings or nothing like that. She could do that stuff now, because she was a ghost.

Charity figured out to give Mom and Dad a gift from her. He was holding the book on his lap. It had been on his bookshelf since he was a little kid. It was about a kid that had died and was telling the mom everything was okay and she didn't have to be sad. Billy thought that was the best idea – ever – and was sitting on his bed trying to get up the courage to do it.

See – one thing Charity didn't know was – it wasn't cool to talk about her anymore – especially about her being a ghost. Mom was still waiting for somebody to find Charity and bring her home, and Dad had just gone nutso; yelling at everybody and such like that. He had this mean look on his face all the time. He even yelled at *Mom* a couple of times, and that was against the rules. (Everybody knows that). Besides, it made her cry, and we were all supposed to be trying not to do that.

Today was good for doing the book thing because it was Sunday and they were going to a church. This Pastor guy – Billy couldn't remember his name – had started coming to see Mom sometimes, and that made Mom ask Dad to go to church. Billy had never been to a church. His friend, Ryan, went every Sunday 'cause he was a Mormon.

Billy got to wear a new pair of pants and this shirt that looked like the ones Dad wore to work. He had even gotten this new belt and grown-up shoes to wear. He thought he looked pretty snazzy. This church idea was good. They were going to be all together in the same place, and if God was around, He would maybe help out. Billy hoped so, anyway, 'cause they could sure use some help.

"Billy! Come on, son. We don't want to be late." Dad was calling from the bottom of the stairs.

Billy took one more look in the bathroom mirror before heading downstairs. He wondered if Charity could see him.

"Okay, Dad. I'm coming!"

Dad was helping Mom with her coat, but they both looked him up and down as he joined them in the foyer. Mom smiled and smoothed his hair a bit.

"My goodness! You look like a full-grown man this morning." Billy struck his best magazine pose and everybody laughed.

"You're looking pretty sharp, there, Billy-boy." Dad said with a smile.

Dad slid into the long, black coat that he wore with suits. Billy thought his own outfit would've looked better with a fancy-guy coat like Dad's, but he pulled on his regular blue and white one that he wore to school all the time because nobody had bought him one of those kind, yet. Maybe by next Sunday he'd have one? He slid the book into the 'secret' inside pocket of his coat and zipped it up.

The car trip was pretty great. They took the old white Impala that Dad called a "Classic." It had blue seats and rode real smooth like he imagined an airplane would feel. Dad had the radio on and Mom was smiling every now and then. Billy's new shoes were hurting already. His white shirt was buttoned all the way up to the very top, and it kinda' felt like he was having a hard time breathing so he kept pulling it away from his throat every couple of minutes. No wonder Dad was mean all the time. Jeez.

"Dad?" He had asked.

"Yes sir? What can I do for you?"

"Are we going to stop for breakfast? I'm hungry."

"Sorry, Billy. We have to get over to the church before their meeting starts, but I'll make you a deal."

"Yeah? What kinda' deal?"

"Well, when I was your age, your Gramma and Grampa always took me to get donuts after church."

"DONUTS!" This had come out louder than he had expected, but, hey, *donuts?* Billy was liking this church thing more all the time. He was shocked when the outburst hadn't earned him any glares or stares from the front seat. Instead, his folks were sharing a little chuckle like in the old days. "Can I get a chocolate milk too?"

"If you behave yourself and sit quietly while Pastor John is giving his sermon, you can even have chocolate milk."

Pastor John, that was his name. "Dad? Is 'John' his first name or his last name?"

"You should ask him." Dad said, just as the Impala swung into the parking lot of the . . .

(Billy read the big white sign with all the swirly wood bits around it) 'Church of Our Savior.' It was a neato building with a steeple and colored glass in the windows and stuff. There were lots of people going inside. They were all dressed up, too. Billy had been relieved to see that, because he didn't want to feel weird. Still, he had felt all fluttery when he got out of the car, so he had taken Mom's hand when she had offered it. Plus, it had seemed like the thing to do for making her happy and all.

11. DEAD OR ALIVE

Charity was fading away. Her world had begun to blur around the edges, and she knew that her time here was growing short. Shasta no longer sought her out for attention, nor did she seem to feel Charity's caresses. Losing that cat had been hard. As long as Charity had been able to interact with a living being -- to comfort and hold and coo over that stupid cat -- she had been able to convince herself that she wasn't really dead.

But I am dead.

Because she could no longer experience fear, the question of what would happen next was more of a cause for wonder than concern. She had convinced herself that her spirit would probably hang around until her body had been discovered, or, perhaps until the Monster had been apprehended. But, it was becoming increasingly clear that those mysteries were for the living to ferret out. That made sense, really. Of what interest were those things to her? Both her body and the Monster had been left behind long ago – and good riddance.

Janice was faring better than she ever had, with new friends and lots of newfound strength and confidence. Billy would be okay. She smiled as she watched him admire his beautiful self in the bathroom mirror. He was a good kid. The only unresolved issues at that point were tangled up around Mom and Dad.

Charity didn't want to leave until her parents were stronger. She was increasingly unsure that the time of her departure was going to be under her control, though. Something had to happen, and happen soonish. She could only hope that a simple gift delivered from a child's hand would somehow be able to unravel all of the complicated turmoil that had snaked its way in and out of their hearts in such a hopeless series of knots and snarls.

When the chubby clergyman had appeared at the front door, Charity had been suspicious. She wondered what he wanted and where he had come from. They had never been 'churchy' people, so she was pretty sure nobody here had invited him. She tried to use her 'ghostly super powers' to look into his soul.

But, I don't have any 'ghostly super powers.' Charity would have sighed then, if she could have. *Death had been such a disappointment.*

Her mother had opened the door with an appropriately puzzled expression.

"Can I help you, um, Father?"

"Pastor John. Nice to meet you. Mrs. Fische?"

"Yes?" She had left him standing on the porch on a cold day in February, which had spoken volumes about her mother's state of being. She didn't trust *anybody* – especially, not uninvited male anybodies. As far as Erica Fische was concerned, all males were suspects in her daughter's disappearance until proven otherwise.

"I serve a small congregation in your community, and we are all aware of your recent loss." He cleared his throat. "I have prayed over whether or not to approach you, as I know that your family is in need of privacy at this time. But, well, it is my calling to reach out to those in need of comfort, and that argument won out every time." He smiled, awkwardly, and his smile had an irresistible, endearing quality.

"He's okay, Mom. Invite the guy in, for heaven's sake!" She laughed at the unintended pun.

"Thank you for coming, Pastor John. We don't belong to any church family at the moment, but. . ."

"Or *ever*. C'mon, Mom, what are you trying to prove?"

"Would you like to come in?"

"Yes, I would. Thank you very much."

They were both smiling now. Charity watched as her mother opened up over the next few hours. Once she had started talking, the words had kept coming. Her hopes, her fears, her feelings of guilt and sadness had all poured out of her – non-stop. Pastor John, to his credit, had not so much as stirred from his place in the brocade armchair. He had leaned forward and listened (and listened, and listened). And there had been something about that silent compassion that had succeeded where everyone else had failed.

Charity didn't know what denomination this guy represented, but she was pretty sure that stuff didn't matter as much as people thought it did. Seemed to her as though anything that brought people together for the purpose of loving one another and easing each other's burdens was a good thing.

In a very short time, this little, round, balding man had won their trust and admiration. It was pretty gutsy to walk up to a stranger's house and ring the bell like that, and a week ago, Pastor John might have been sent packing.

Maybe it was just time.

Mom had been shocked to look up and see where the hands were on the grandfather clock. Charity could see her wheels turning and it made her laugh out loud. Mom had been going on for hours, and it was coming up on 6:00 p.m. Should she invite Pastor John to dinner?

Did they have anything in the house that even resembled dinner? Dad and Billy would be coming through the door from soccer practice any time now, and she couldn't count on her husband to be tactful.

"Well, I am so happy to have had this opportunity to get to know you better." He said, graciously, as he moved towards the door. "But, I really must be on my way."

"Oh. Must you, really? I feel awful about yammering on at you all this time. I had no idea it was so late!"

"Mrs. Fische, if I have been able to ease your suffering in any small way, then I consider myself blessed." He had looked down and shuffled his feet, and that posture of natural humility had taken the 'churchiness' out of it. Charity liked this guy a lot.

"Yes. Yes. You truly have." Mom was saying as she fetched his coat from the closet. "I must have needed to yammer on at someone in the worst way." Her smile took years away from her face and Charity was reminded of the way her Mama used to be.

Charity found herself on the porch and had watched him walk away. He had a Charlie Chaplain mode of locomotion that brought another smile to her face.

God bless you, Pastor John. Charity mused as she leaned against the porch rail.

12. OUR GUY

Homicide detectives Robbins and Slade were spending their day in an unmarked Ford Taurus. They were parked in front of a row of dilapidated townhomes in Laurel, Maryland. Across the street, a dark green Ford truck was crouching ominously in a cracked and oil-spotted driveway. It hadn't moved in days.

"What does this guy do for a living?" Robbins asked between bites of turkey sandwich.

"Got me." Detective Slade answered. "According to his file, he hasn't held a job since June of last year. Construction. Just up and quit one day and never came back."

"So? What? Do you think he's on the dole?"

"Probably." Slade tapped the steering wheel impatiently. "We have got to get in there! I know this is our guy. There are a lot of people who would like to get their hands on him, and I'm one of them."

"Yeah. That poor kid. Imagine how scared she must have been. Did you get a look at his face?"

"Like the friggin' Boogie Man meets Freddie Kruger. I know."

"And built like the Hoover Dam."

"She didn't have a chance in hell. Not a chance. Pretty little thing, too. I mean; not a beauty, really, but innocent and . . . you know."

"Yep. Beauty and the Beast." They looked at the truck in unison. "Well, he's got to come out sooner or later." Matthew Robbins finished off his sandwich and licked some mustard off his thumb. "What do you say we make a case for taking that tarp out of the back of his truck? Think we could get a warrant?"

"Not without clueing him in on the entire investigation. Nope. Our instructions are to wait and watch. Watch and wait."

"I'm betting there's all kind of DNA in that tarp; probably enough to solve cases from DC to VA." He grabbed the front and back panels of a bag of chips and pulled. "Want some?"

"No thanks, man. Cholesterol. Just wait until you get to be my age. That's when all the fun stops." Detective Slade checked his reflection in the rearview. He'd already found a few gray strands mixed in with his dark, wavy hair. And, there wasn't anywhere near as much of that as there used to be, either. He scanned Matt's lean and youthful appearance and wondered how he managed to stay slim on a diet like that.

Matt crunched a handful of potato chips and reached in for another handful. "Then I'd better enjoy the hell out of it now, right?"

"Go for it. Just don't say I didn't warn you." Len took another swig from his warm can of Diet Coke. *Ick. Pack a cooler next time. Live and learn.*

"'Dwight.' You ask me, this dude turns out to be our killer, then it was his parents' fault for naming him that in the first place."

"It's a name. I'm not one to poke fun at other people's names, being a 'Leonard,' myself."

"Hey! Leonard's okay. I've known lots of Leonard's and there's not one axe murderer or sexual deviate among them."

They laughed.

"What the fuck happened to his face? What? Was he run over by a lawn tractor as a child? Talk about being hit by the ugly stick." Matt wiped a hand absentmindedly on his jeans.

"All I know is that, besides matching our profile to a tee, he was living in VA when the girl disappeared. All of a sudden he gets an urge to leave town? I've got a feeling about this one. He's our guy."

"Never been down for murder, though, only a few sexual assaults and one rape conviction that was overturned."

"Maybe he's figured out what they all do, eventually -- that the best way to stay out of jail is to destroy the evidence."

"Know what? I'm starting to wonder if he's even in there. What if he ditched the truck and climbed out a back window or something? I mean, no lights, no television, doesn't leave the house for days. What's he doing in there?"

"He's in there. Just hold your horses. We wait and we watch." Slade said this last with a tone of finality.

The sullen crunching of chips and rattling of cellophane echoed in the new silence between them. The day had stretched out into a series of very long, uneventful minutes as the homicide detectives watched and waited.

13. PONYTAILS

Winter again; the Monster gathered his victim's hair and cut it off close to her scalp. His own hair, long, light brown and curly, had been tied up to keep it out of the way as he worked. The blue eyes that had always been his best feature had gone an intense slate grey to match his level of concentration. By dipping the freshly-cut ends into a special mixture of resin, he was able to keep all of the precious strands together in a silky ponytail. As the resin took hold, he gloried over this latest addition to his collection. Her hair had been wavy and an unusual shade of auburn that had caught the sunlight (and his rapt attention) from the very first moment.

He stroked the red-gold hair; held it up to his freshly-shaved cheek and reveled in the softness of it. It was the memories and these treasured tokens that would help to quell the flames of his desire until some new quarry could offer herself up.

He had seen her leaving the 7-11 after dark with a gallon of milk. It was a Wednesday, and he watched as she ducked behind the dumpsters and into some woods. Curious, he had waited a few minutes before walking over to investigate her route: A well-worn footpath that wound its way through a wooded area and eventually opened into a comfortable neighborhood full of well-groomed lawns and upper-middle class homes. He could tell by the way she walked that she was going to be a good time. Her innocence had beckoned to him with each carefree stride.

The following Wednesday night – *yes, indeedy* – there she was again. Being a good girl and making the weekly milk run. He had waited for her to enter the store and then taken up his position behind the dumpster. The rest had been easy. He smiled and ran his hand over one bulging bicep.

Women turned their heads to watch him pass by. Tall, muscular and fit – he could turn his charm on and off again in the time it took to flash his crooked smile. His looks had always gotten him whatever he wanted, but, when it came time to "do the deed," his pecker hadn't been up for it. As a result, the Monster had learned how to turn away admirers – male or female – before anything got too serious.

I don't like stale bread, either. Gimme' a fresh, buttered roll – warm from the oven – every time.

He hadn't known her name until he'd seen her angelic little face smiling back at him from the television the next day. "Amy." It suited her. What a sweet little morsel she had been. Not for the first time, he was sorry that he couldn't keep them; but then promptly shook it off.

Just not worth the risk. What a shame.

Decomposition had already begun to take hold of her little body, and the smell was corrupt and revolting. He hated the smell; hated the bodies and all the work they made for him. He didn't want to have to kill them at all, but this country's backward legal system had refused to acknowledge and make provision for his needs. Someday he would move to a country where they paid young girls to give it up; then, they could to their job – get some spending cash -- and just go on living their little lives. Why should he do jail time just because he liked 'em young when business men in Japan, Korea, and parts of Europe got it on the way home from work every evening for a few Yen or a measly handful of Euros?

Lots of men like 'em young and tight.

Memories of her appreciative moans had made him grow hard again. She had squeaked like a mouse when he grabbed her. Milk had hit the dirt and gone everywhere, enveloping them in the arousing smell of wet earth and adding a charming 'explosion' to the moment. This time, he wouldn't leave anything behind. The umbrella had been a mistake; not because he had touched it or nothing. The problem with the umbrella was it had given the cops a place to search.

Ten years behind bars. *Ten years*. And, for what? He hadn't even hurt the kid! Just touched her pretty panties and held her by the hair until she licked where he told her to. That had been ten years to get strong; to help him accept himself and become convinced that he should assert his manly rights. He wasn't gonna' settle for diddlin' when he deserved more. Fulfilling their sexual needs was what men did. Now, it was his turn.

After laying his new trophy carefully into place beside the others, the Monster picked up his hunting knife and set to work disassembling 12 yr-old Amy Kendall.

What was the matter with parents nowadays, anyway? They let these girls wander the streets at night – even though it was all over the news about the missing ones. He hoped they would feel plenty guilty for neglecting their god-given stewardship. Why did people even have children if they were just going to dangle them out there for people like me?

Little Amy was face down. He didn't like them looking at him while he worked. It made him sad – it really did. Their heads came off easier that way, too.

'Course, they were cut clean through on the other side already.

What kind of judicial system would make this horrifying carnage necessary? They hadn't given him any other choice, had they? What was he supposed to do? Stay celibate? He was a man and he had a man's needs. As each tender bone separated under his knife, his resentment grew. This was THEIR fault. They made him do this.

Goddamn government fairies. Who did they think they were fooling? The half that wasn't bending over little boys was paying out money for cheap whores and peep shows. The trick was to never get caught. He knew that now. No witnesses.

Amy Kendall's head had rolled away from her little body as soon as the neck bones had been severed. The Monster clutched her bangs and, without hesitation, flung her terrified and bloodied face into the barrel of lime that had been standing by. One by one, the remaining ragged-edged bits were layered in and covered up until the barrel could be sealed tight and rolled away for storage.

14. HUNG JURY

The parents of teens throughout Maryland and Virginia had been tuning in to watch the six o'clock news every night since the "Shortcut Stalker" had begun his rampage. Four girls, aged 12 – 16 had gone missing from trails near their homes. All had disappeared without a trace – with the exception of the first; a Charity Fische from Fredericksburg, VA.

Detectives Robbins and Slade had been called away from their stake-out detail when it became clear that Dwight T. Genakowski was not their man, after all. Apparently, Mr. Genakowski had been intensely aware of their surveillance, however. For, after having received numerous complaints about a nasty odor coming from the townhome, the landlord let himself in to find poor Dwight hanging from a beam in the basement. He had a note pinned to his shirt pocket that said "I ain't done nuthin to no kid."

The convenience store staff had all been interviewed, but nobody had seen anything suspicious the night that Amy had disappeared. The 7-11 surveillance system had been recently updated, so Amy's image on the tape had been surprisingly clear. There had only been two women and a child in the store that night, and – though all three had been located and interviewed – nobody could report having seen anything or anyone out of the ordinary.

The youngest victim, to date, twelve-year-old Amy Kendall had been wearing a green and white coat, jeans and a pair of silver, pink and white Skecher tennis shoes. Her hair was long and she had pushed it back behind one ear just before reaching into the refrigerator unit and pulling out a gallon of fat-free milk. Looking bored, she had hefted it onto the counter and paid the clerk with a ten-dollar bill. Then, she had smiled at the clerk, said "Thanks," and shoved the change into her coat pocket before grabbing the hefty jug and pushing her way out of the store one-handed.

The tape had been called "haunting," and was broadcast on both local and national news. It would prove to be the last anyone would ever see of Amy. The public was up in arms and the FBI was called in to take over the investigation.

Agents Trask and Harter of the FBI were dispatched to re-examine all of the evidence and question everyone involved as if for the first time. They needed to find the pieces to this puzzle that others might have missed. Their first stop on that journey was at the home of Janice Schuster – the last person to have seen Charity Fische alive.

The house was a rancher-style, probably built in the late 80's. Harter pulled into the driveway and shut off the engine. They were expected, and a tall blonde teenager was waiting for them at the front door before they had even had an opportunity to knock.

"Please come in." She said, eagerly. "We are so glad that you guys are on this case!"

They had barely gotten through the door when they were joined by an older, heavyset woman with tightly curled and sprayed salt and pepper hair. Her perfume was overpowering and her nails were long and bright red with wild white and black flowers painted in the middle of each.

"Mrs. Shuster?" This was Harter, as he could see his partner was trying not to choke in the fumes.

"Yes! Stephanie Schuster. So glad you could come. Charity was Janice's best friend in the world and her death has been just unbearable for all of us."

The agents exchanged glances. *Her death?*

"Where would you like to do this?" Mrs. Schuster asked. "Around the kitchen table, or in the living room?"

"Wherever you prefer, would be just fine." Trask piped up for the first time. "How about right here?"

As they were standing within a few feet of the living room sofa, Mrs. Shuster waved them into the room and offered them a seat.

"Coffee? Tea? I have sodas, too."

"No. Thank you. We have just come from dinner at the hotel. Could we just ask you a few questions? We know that you've answered them all before, but would appreciate your patience. We are new to the investigation and want to look at everything with fresh eyes."

"Oh. Certainly! We are happy to help in any way; any way at all."

Janice was the last to sit down. She pulled a chair in from the dining room and sat there clasping and un-clasping her hands with apparent anxiety.

"Thank you. Now, a few minutes ago, you referred to Charity's 'death?' Do you have any reason to believe that she is no longer alive?" This question was directed to both of them, but Trask's eyes were locked on Janice.

"I know that she is dead. I don't know how I know – I just do." Janice said.

Her mother, realizing how this might be perceived, spoke quickly and emphatically. "You see, they have been friends since they started kindergarten. When I say 'friends,' I mean more like sisters. Both girls were – how do I say this – unusual. I mean to say that they didn't exactly fit in with their peers. . ." She looked uncomfortable.

"We were misfits, nerds, whatever labels kids give the unpopular crowd. But, Charity and I were okay with that. We had each other. Those kids didn't matter. We were as close as friends could ever be, and the night she was taken, I knew right away that she wasn't ever coming back." A tear ran down Janice's face. "My heart was broken. I just knew."

"Okay. We've got the picture." Trask continued. "What was Charity doing here on the night that she disappeared?"

"Well, that's my bridge night, you see, and. . . " Janice spoke over her mother's explanation.

"We always watched the show 'True Blood' together on Thursday nights while Mom was out. We would have cookies and chips, watch the show, then, she would head back home around 10:00."

"This was every Thursday?"

"Yes. Well, during the program season. I think there are like 8 episodes each season? I haven't watched it . . . since. . ."

"So, to the best of your recollection, Charity left your house shortly after 10:00 p.m."

"Yes. She always called her mother to let her know she was starting for home."

"Did Charity have a cell phone?"

"No. Her parents didn't believe in giving kids phones. She called from our kitchen phone."

"And, she talked to her mother at that time?"

"No. Her mom didn't pick up, but Charity left a message."

"Okay. The umbrella that was found at the crime scene was yours, correct?"

"Yes. The rain was really coming down when she left, so she asked me for an umbrella and I gave her that one."

"As far as you know she was headed home?"

"Yes. Totally. It was really nasty outside and it was dark. She would have probably run all the way. We didn't have any other friends – or boyfriends, so she would have gone straight home."

Agent Harter raised an eyebrow and made a note.

"We both like boys – don't get that mixed up – they just didn't pay any attention to us because . . . you know . . . we weren't . . . um . . . pretty enough."

Harter nodded and crossed out his last note.

"Janice, would you be willing to show us the shortcut that Charity took that night?"

"Yes. Of course. Let me get my coat."

Agent Trask picked up a framed photo from the end table. "Isn't this a photo of Charity Fische?" He asked.

Mrs. Schuster nodded.

"Who is that girl sitting next to her?"

"Hmm?" She looked at the photo again, perplexed. "Why that's Janice, of course." She said.

Agents Trask and Harter looked from the photograph to the young woman that was pulling on her coat in the foyer.

"I can see the resemblance now." Trask said. "She has lost a lot of weight, and her hair was *red*?"

"Oh! Yes." Mrs. Schuster stood – her ghastly perfume wafting with every movement. "This whole incident has been such a shock for Janice, you know. She stopped eating, and . . . well, she has changed a good bit over the last year, hasn't she?"

For the first time, Janice's story made sense. The girl in the photo looked the part of the nerdy outcast, where the girl they had just interviewed had not.

The tall blonde adolescent came forward with their coats, and Agents Trask and Harter bid goodnight to Mrs. Schuster before accompanying Janice to the scene of the first abduction.

15. FREEDOM FROM SPEECHES

The church was filled with long wooden benches that had high backs. His mom had pulled him into the 2nd to last row with Dad on the aisle. It was nice to be sandwiched between them. It felt safe and he wasn't feeling all sick to his stomach anymore. One of the first things that happened was a long prayer. Billy knew he was supposed to bow his head and keep his eyes closed like everybody else, but he had wanted to look around some more.

Mom was wearing her best blue dress. It had a shiny black belt that made her look like a movie star. She had pulled her brown hair up into a bun and put a decoration on it. With her eyes closed, he could see the makeup on her eyelids that was the same blue as her dress. He thought she looked very pretty. Dad looked good, too. He even *smelled* good. Everybody said he looked like his Dad, so that was okay.

A baby cried for just a moment and Billy tried to see where the sound had come from. He didn't see any babies or even any kids back here where they were sitting. Sounds kinda' echoed in the church, though, and it was probably up front somewhere. He figured it's mother had probably given it a bottle or toy or something to shut it up.

On the back of every bench was a place to put green church books. They looked kinda' old and each one had the same cross on the front in shiny gold – some shinier than others. He looked up front at Pastor John standing behind a wooden thing with a microphone on it so everybody could hear him pray. There was a huge gold-colored cross hanging on the wall behind him with special lights shining on it.

Billy wondered if all the prayers were gonna' be this long or if the Pastor was just showing off for his folks.

"And we pray these things to God's glory! Amen, and Amen."

Pastor John had a deep voice for such a little guy. Even Billy knew that "Amen" meant the prayer was over. He pulled his hand out of his mother's and reached for one of the green books to see what they looked like inside. Mom let him take it and open it up, but she made a "shhh!" face with her finger.

As quietly as he could, he opened the book and flipped through it. It was all music like they gave him for the Holiday Program at school. Billy closed it and put it back. He noticed that there were a lot of old people there. The people that were sitting right in front of their row had grey hair in different shades, and some of the ladies had hats on.

Just when his bottom was hurting from all the sitting, everybody stood up at once and grabbed a green book. Billy jumped up and grabbed one, too. Then Mom and Dad were singing together, just like they used to do on long car trips, and around the campfire, and sometimes when they watched stupid old movies with people singing in them. He didn't know this song, so he just held his book up and moved his head and lips around so people would think he was smart too.

In between the singing parts, there was another long part where Pastor John talked. There hadn't been a clock anywhere, but Billy figured it must be dinner time by now, and he still hadn't had *breakfast*. A lady that looked Mom's age got up to read the bible for a while, too. He wondered if they could have the donuts for dinner?

The good thing that happened was when he had started to fidget around and get whiney, Mom and Dad had both taken one of his hands and *smiled* – all three of them holding hands – like a family. Now, he couldn't wait to give them Charity's present! He had closed his eyes and thought a message to her as loud as he could.

"Look, Charity! We are going to be okay! Mom and Dad are holding hands and singing! We are going to get donuts and chocolate milk and I'm gonna' give them your present and everything will be good again!"

But, Charity wasn't there.

16. THE FACE OF EVIL

Something evil was moving slowly down the street towards her house. Charity had just watched her family drive off in the white Impala when she had been overcome with a sense of foreboding. The slow-moving truck was as ominous as a large shark gliding gracefully past the occupants of a very small raft.

It was the Monster. She had never seen his face, but there had been no doubt of his identity. In place of the fear that she could no longer feel, suspicion and curiosity had taken hold. Charity found herself in the passenger seat of his truck, which was moving stealthily through the neighborhood towards the woods.

She examined his profile for the first time. His light brown hair had been pulled back neatly into a long ponytail. He had a high forehead, long, straight nose and well-formed ears. He didn't look like a monster at all. He must have felt her staring because he started to look around nervously, and she could smell his sweat.

The Monster reached for his beer and took several swallows before wiping his mouth with the back of his callused hand. He had been wearing one of those quilted vests over a flannel shirt, and the shirtsleeves had been stretched tightly over the muscles of his arms.

"What are you doing here?" Charity demanded. "You get away from here and you don't come back!"

He had turned his blue eyes towards her for a moment and she had seen nothing but a predator in them; the pitiless eyes of a cobra, a panther or a shark.

He had gulped down the last of his beer then, and tossed the empty can on the floor at her feet. Angry, Charity stomped it flat. The crushing sound had been satisfyingly loud and the truck had veered crazily to the right and pulled to a stop. The Monster looked at his newly-flattened beer can; never taking his foot off of the brakes.

"What the fuck?" He put the truck into park and reached down to pick up the flattened can. He examined it carefully and tossed it to the dash. Wiping the sweat off his face with his sleeve, the Monster got out and walked around to search under her seat. "What the holy fuck was that?"

Charity retrieved the flattened can from the dashboard and pelted the Monster in the head with it. His hands flew to his face and he turned to look down at the can in horror.

"What the holy-mother-of-fuck is going on here?!"

"You get out of here and you don't come back – EVER! I know who you are and I know what you did and I'm watching you!" Charity reached over and put the car into drive, then flashed over to the sidewalk to watch the ensuing craziness.

He had yelped when he realized what was happening and had grabbed the open passenger door to hold on. This had only succeeded in dragging him mercilessly down the hill a good way before he had finally decided to let go. Being without a driver, the Ford hadn't curved when the road had. Instead, it had rammed into Mr. Napp's shiny black 350Z. The resulting momentum nudged both vehicles into the waiting arms of Mrs. Stanish's naked pink dogwood tree.

It being early Sunday morning when just about everybody was home for the day, it had only taken a few moments for the crowd to begin to form. The Monster turned away from the accident and ducked behind the nearest house. He did not want to be caught in this area. Neither did he wish to answer a lot of questions about what he had been doing there.

The truck would be linked to him at his Silver Spring, Maryland address. A quick background check would put him smack-dab in the "Shortcut Stalker" suspect list and his properties would be thoroughly searched.

"Goddamnit! Fuck! Fuck!"

The Monster considered walking down to the accident scene. He could say that he had put the truck in park to make a delivery and the brake must have disengaged or failed. But, what if somebody had already called the police? No. He had to get out of there – fast – and his wallet was still in the truck.

"What the holy fuck is happening to me?"

Charity gleefully snuck up behind him and pelted him in the head with the beer can.

One more time, for luck.

17.DONUTS

Billy tugged off his coat in the donut shop and sat down. It had been hot in there after being outside. When his mom and dad joined him at the little table, they had bags and drinks in their hands.   It had only been 10:00 in the morning when they had left the church and that had been a huge surprise because the talking had seemed to go on forever and ever. Anyway, he was *starving*!

Pastor John had stood in the fancy double doors to keep people from running out, and he had been shaking everybody's hands and talking some more. When Billy's parents had started to talk back about how much they enjoyed his sermon and stuff, he had tugged on his Dad's sleeve as if to say, *"Jeez, alright already. Let's go!"* His Dad had patted him on the hand and given him that look that says, "Keep your pants on, son! We'll be leaving in a minute!"

The donut shop was on the other side of town, so the drive had seemed to take a very long time. Plus, he was anxious to fulfill his promise to Charity.

"What kind of donuts are you going to get this morning?" His mom had asked.

"I dunno yet." Billy thought about all the different kinds of donuts, and pretty much wanted all of them, but said, "I think I'll have the chocolate frosted and one of the just glazed ones."

"That sounds yummy," said his mom. "I'm going to get the biggest cup of coffee that they have."

"C'mon, Mom. Don't you want your cinnamon bun? You always get your cinnamon bun."

"Maybe. You know what? I think I will. All that religion made me hungry." She smiled, and he had loved the way it had made her look younger – like magic.

Daddy had chimed in at that. "Well, if you guys are going to pig out, then I guess I'll have a breakfast sandwich and a donut, myself!"

"Dad?"

"Uh huh?"

"Can we get donuts every Sunday?"

"We'll see, Billy. We'll see."

The shop had all glass in the front so people could see all the donuts on display and get hungry for 'em. There was a long line up to the counter and Billy had groaned with impatience. It smelled like coffee and cake. People were asking for donuts and trying to make the store people understand, 'cause they didn't speak English too good. Mostly, it worked when people just pointed at the ones they wanted.

"Go on over there and save us a table, son," His dad had said. "See the napkins over on that counter? Why don't you get some and spread them out so we can put our food on them. See? The line is moving pretty fast."

Maybe they thought the line had been moving pretty good, but it had been just more waiting for Billy, and he was way tired of waiting. He had been excited to finally see them walking over with the bulging white paper bags in their hands.

"Okay, Billy. Yours were the chocolate frosted and the regular glazed donut, right?"

"Mmm!" He said, reaching to arrange his donuts on the napkin that he had spread out like a plate. "And, my..."

"And, here's your chocolate milk."

"Yay!" He took a big bite of the chocolate donut and licked the frosting off his fingers before struggling to open the milk container.

Mom was stirring some stuff into her coffee, and Dad had gotten himself a bottle of strawberry-flavored milk to go with his breakfast sandwich, so he set to twisting the top off of that. The eggs and bacon on his sandwich smelled so good that Billy started to wish he had ordered one of those, instead. Dad's coconut frosting was looking pretty tasty, too. Maybe he would order that next Sunday.

"Okay. Mom? Dad?" Billy waited until he had his parents' attention. "I know you won't believe me, but I promised I'd tell you about what happened and give you something."

His mom and dad had exchanged puzzled looks. "Okay. Go ahead, Billy. We promise to listen, Right, honey?" Dad had taken mom's hand and was holding it tight.

"I know you never believed me about talking to Charity – don't say nuthin' 'cause I know. But, she did talk to me that night, and I saw her – just like for real. Okay. So, a couple nights ago, my light goes on real late, and I *knew* it was her. I couldn't see her and I couldn't hear her this time, so I said like, "Is that you, Charity?" So, then she picked up that white poodle that I have that used to be on her bed – 'member mom?"

His mother nodded, then looked down. She seemed sad, but he kept going, because he had promised Charity that he would.

"So, then I knew it was Charity – even though I couldn't see her this time. The next thing she did was get something out of my bookcase and put it right into my hands! It looked like it was floating right to me, but I knew she was bringing it, so I wasn't scared or nuthin'."

Encouraged by the lack of interruption and the way his parents were paying attention to him this time, Billy pulled his coat off of the back of his chair and dug into the 'secret' inside pocket to bring out the book.

"I couldn't hear her this time – like I said, but I told her that I would give it to you, Mom, and she was happy, 'cause that was what she wanted me to do. She even pulled up my blankets and turned out the light. God's honest truth – and I just came from church and all. . ."

Billy handed the little book to his mother. She had let go of Dad and taken it carefully in both hands. When she read the title "I'm Okay, Mommy," she had begun to cry. But, this time it had been a different kind of tears. Billy had reached his arms up to hug his mother tight. His Dad had wrapped his arms around both of them, and – for the smallest of moments – the Fisches had known peace.

18. RUNNING ON EMPTY

Jonathan Emile Garrett, ('Jack' to anyone who wanted to stay on his good side), cut through back yards until he reached the destination that he had started for that morning; the very trail where he had taken his first plaything the year before. This time, instead of being a confident stalker in search of prey, he was a fugitive on the run. The path had taken him quickly to a less-affluent community closer to the center of town. There had been a bus stop near the trail's exit where he had considered waiting for the next bus before remembering that he had no cash, coins or cards.

My fucking wallet is in my fucking truck on that fucking street surrounded by fucking cops.

His only option at that point was to walk the eight or nine blocks to the shopping mall and try to catch a taxi from there to his sister's house. She still lived in Virginia, would be home today, and probably wouldn't hesitate to pay his fare. What he was going to do after that, he didn't know.

I have no keys, no identification, no cash, and no clothes. My face is going to be all over the news tonight. Fuck!

The sidewalks were bordered by identical cracker-box houses, dead shrubbery and frost-covered yards. It had been a brisk morning, and he thought it might snow. Though it had been early February, several homes still wore their shabby Christmas regalia. Poverty was depressing.

Jack wondered whether or not he could trust Eileen. Wouldn't she turn him in to the authorities when she found out what he was wanted for? What about her redneck husband and their kid? His 'activities' had been front-page news for so long that everybody across three states wanted to see him on death row.

If I killed them – killed all three of them – I could take a car, credit cards, jewelry . . .

A young couple had just driven up to one of the houses and begun to unload a toddler and some groceries. The woman eyed him, suspiciously. His heart was beating furiously as he tried to be cool and look away.

I can't kill everybody.

He tried to get control of his pulse rate; breathing in through his nose and out through his mouth the way he did at the gym. The one thing he couldn't think about – not ever – was that flattened beer can. No rational explanation could be made for what had happened that morning. He preferred to think it had been some kind of hallucination brought on by lack of sleep, indigestion or his overwhelming desire for his next 'toy.'

It wasn't a ghost. Not that girl's ghost, come to get him back for what he had done to her. Jack forced his thoughts away from that notion before it had a chance to take hold.

Perhaps he was just crazy? Weren't serial killers and rapists supposed to be a few feathers shy of a whole duck? Maybe he had been getting increasingly psychotic with each sweet child that he had been forced to destroy? All of that gory sawing and stacking. Their faces. He shuddered.

I didn't want to do that part. I never wanted to kill them. There had been no choice! It wasn't my fault. I thought they were so pretty and fresh. I would've kept them. . .would have loved them.

He tried to imagine slitting Eileen's throat and couldn't. His big sister, she had always been the one he could depend on. He could remember her reading to him when he had the chicken pox, and sticking up for him when kids called him a wimp because of his scrawny, pale body. Prison had made him what he was now; strong, muscular, nobody's patsy.

Maybe I can just tie them up and take off. Once I'm headed for parts unknown, it won't matter what they tell the cops.

Each step brought him closer to his customary calm. It was a pleasant walk, after all, and nobody was even looking for him yet. He had time. Besides, the "Shortcut Stalker" had always been able to outsmart the cops, and there was no reason to believe that he couldn't just keep on outsmarting them.

The first thing I'm going to do is cut off all this hair. Maybe dye it? Eileen dyes her hair; probably has a box or two around the house. Or, maybe I'll shave my head? I'd probably look slick with a shaved head.

He turned the last corner and headed towards the JC Penney's entrance of the local mall. It shouldn't be too hard to find a phone here. He needed to get his shit together and put some serious miles between him and this whole goddamn town.

It wasn't a ghost. There aren't any ghosts. I'm just going crazy, that's all. Nothing to worry about; lots of people are crazy. Beer cans don't flatten themselves. Beer cans don't attack. Get a grip.

Jack E. Garrett was no wimp. And, if he was crazy, then he was crazy like a fox. Jack's eyes glittered with predatory calm as he crossed the parking lot, and his confident strides turned heads.

19. LIGHTS, CAMERA, ACTION

Dan Fische knew something was wrong the minute they turned onto Chandler from Vine. It looked as though every police cruiser in Virginia had been called to this location. He could see five parked end-to-end with their lights rolling, but sensed the activity continued on down the hill.

"Wonder what's going on?" He said. "Look at them! There must be a dozen or more."

"Do you think they could have caught him?"

"No. This has got to be something else. I doubt our guy would come back to this neighborhood."

"Is it a burglering?" Billy unfastened his seatbelt and jumped up to look out the window. "Did people get stabbed and stuff?"

"Billy. You come in the house with me. It could be dangerous. Dan? Would you check out the house first, and then give Ron a call? Everything seems to be happening down there on his block. Maybe he can tell us what's what."

"I'll just walk down there, once I get you guys safe inside."

"Aw! Can I come, too! Please, Dad?" This was the most exciting thing that had happened since. . . Billy thought about the night Charity had gone missing and felt sick.

"Billy. Come inside, please. Now."

"Dad? It's gotta' be safe with all these police guys around? Please?"

"Billy. Now." Erica had been standing on the front porch with her arms crossed. She was not going to back down on this one.

Once he had made sure that his wife and son were safely locked inside the house, Dan started down the hill towards the source of all the commotion. A press van pulled up as he arrived at the accident scene and a reporter jumped out and accosted Dan with a microphone. The camera team was on the ground and rolling before the journalist could even get a word out.

"Mr. Fische? You are Mr. Daniel Fische; father of Charity – the young girl that was abducted last year by the Shortcut Stalker?"

"Yes. I am Dan Fische. What is this about? What has happened here?"

It was then that Dan had noticed the wrecked green Ford F150. "Did they catch him? Is that bastard in custody? What happened?"

The reporter turned to address the camera. "We are on location where the truck, believed to belong to the Shortcut Stalker has been discovered just blocks from where he took his first known victim – Charity Fische. Daniel Fische, the girl's father, has just arrived and has not yet heard the news. Mr. Fische, how does it feel to know that the man responsible for abducting your daughter may have been identified?"

"Oh my God." Viewers all over the nation watched as the color drained from Dan's face and he turned to join the officers that had gathered on the far side of the damaged truck. He was clearly overwhelmed and unsteady on his feet, and the cameras zoomed in tight so as not to miss a possible stumble, fall or faint. Revolving lights of blue, red and green were stirring the contents of his stomach like an electric mixer.

I can't faint. I can't fall. I can't show emotion. I must be strong. I must not vomit. The world is watching. He may be watching. . .

The first few flakes of snow had been drifting down to melt upon the scene. They were large and wet, and had touched Dan's face with soft, cool caresses. The gentle play of snowflakes had made a peaceful counterpart to the flashing lights and bursts of radio chatter. Tow trucks had just arrived and had been moving into position to pull the vehicles apart. A fingerprint team was going over the interior of the truck. People moved like bees on a hive. Dan was putting one foot in front of the other as everything around him seemed to be spinning in slow motion. One of the detectives had recognized him and was waving him into their circle. He focused on the detective with every last ounce of his will and had moved forward with an unfathomable slowness; as though he had been moving knee-deep through molasses.

"Here comes Mr. Fische. Let's fill him in on everything." Detective Trask waved to Mr. Fische and called one of the officers over. "Howard? Please get those reporters behind a barrier of some sort? Tell them we'll be over to give them a statement in a few minutes."

"I'm on it. Want me to set up the perimeter one block down in either direction?"

"Hold them back two blocks for this one. Try to get the neighbors back inside too. Whitley?" He had called to another officer. "Go with him and get this area taped off, will you?"

A pretty African American woman from the forensic team joined the group of agents holding a man's wallet in her gloved hands. "Wallet and I.D., sir. It's all here. The truck was owned by one 'Jonathan E. Garrett' of Silver Spring, MD. Good looking son-of-a-bitch, too."

"Jesus. Sure doesn't look the type, does he? That man could have any woman he wanted, and he takes kids."

"We've got him, now, sir; name, photo, address, bank accounts; the whole enchilada."

"Davis, ran him through CODA and this guy is a good fit for our perpetrator. Well, it might not be our guy, but this certainly puts Mr. Garrett at the top of the list."

Dan heard a word here, or there, but it wasn't long before the broad swath of voices had woven themselves into a heavy, buzzing blanket of sound had folded around his body just before the ground had come up to meet him and everything had faded to black.

Zoom lenses had been universally employed to catch the action. The headlines would read: "Father of Victim Collapses at Discovery of Villain's Identity."

"Nationwide Manhunt is Underway for Shortcut Stalker"

"Father Overwhelmed as Police Prepare to Release Photo of Shortcut Stalker"

20. LOST AND FOUND

Janice had been folding laundry in the family room when the big news broke. The classic movie she had been watching had just started to get good when the "News Flash" banner had come across the screen.

"Oh, crap. Now I'm going to miss the best part."

Her disappointment had been short-lived, however. When Charity's Dad had filled the screen and she had heard enough to get excited, she hollered for her mother.

"Mom! Mom! Come here! They've found the guy! Mom!"

Mrs. Schuster had been busy putting their Sunday dinner together, but she washed her hands and was still clutching a handful of paper towels when she joined Janice in front of the set.

"What's all this yelling about? Is that Dan Fische? What's going on?"

"Wow. I know where they are! See that? That's Mr. Napp's house. They're right down the street from Charity's . . . I mean. . ."

"Shh! I can't hear what they're saying. Turn it up."

"We are on location where the truck, believed to belong to the Shortcut Stalker has been discovered just blocks from where he took his first known victim – Charity Fische. Daniel Fische, the girl's father, has just arrived and has not yet heard the news. Mr. Fische, how does it feel to know that the man responsible for abducting your daughter may have been identified?"

"Oh my God."

"Well, it's about time." Janice complained through her excitement and relief. "It only took you guys a year." She bit the pinky nail of her right hand

"He doesn't look so good, does he? Poor man. Looks like he walked into that mess blind."

"Hey. Where's Mrs. Fische? Do you think she knows yet?"

Stephanie Schuster ran into the kitchen and picked up the phone.

"Erica? Do you have your television on? Turn it on! They've got the guy's truck! They know who he is!"

"What? Do they have him in custody? Who is he?" Erica dropped the receiver and rushed to turn on the TV.

"Erica? Hello?" Then to Janice, "I think she has gone to turn her television on. Yep. I can hear it in the background."

There had been a collective "No!" followed shortly by an "Oh my God!" when the camera had zoomed in on Dan's collapse. He had folded like a marionette that had been tossed aside by a bored child.

"Erica? Are you there?" Stephanie put the receiver down after having heard the resolute slamming of Erica's front door. "Janice. Get your coat! We're going over there."

They had opted for the car, even though walking would have been a shorter route, because Mrs. Schuster's knees, ankles and feet (not to mention an extra 75 lbs. or so) would have slowed them down considerably. Unfortunately, the road had been closed down and they had ended up having to walk several blocks anyway.

Dan had still not regained consciousness by the time Erica had arrived on the scene. She had pushed her way past neighbors, newscasters, policemen and paramedics to find him lying on his back with a silver foil sheet wrapped around him.

"Please. I'm his wife. Excuse me." She pushed through and knelt on the lawn amid the freshly-falling snowflakes and touched his face – not giving a thought to her best dress. "Dan? Dan?" She took both his hands in hers.

"Ma'am. I'm sorry, Ma'am, but I'm going to have to ask you to move aside so we can help your husband." The paramedic had put a hand on her shoulder. She had shrugged him off.

Dan's eyes had come open at that moment and had found hers. He had looked confused for a second or two before sitting up with a start. "They know who took our baby, he sobbed. They know his name and what he looks like and where he lives. . ." His words had been meant for her alone, but the nation would hear them repeated again and again. The embrace and the tears that they had shared in that intimate moment of joy, grief, victory and loss were to be viewed world-wide throughout the ensuing manhunt and for years afterward.

The Monster stood in front of a bank of flat-screen televisions in the Best Buy store at the mall. He had watched the tender scene from a dozen different angles, simultaneously. Shoppers had started to gather around him and a celebratory mood was taking hold.

"What's going on?" A woman with two toddlers and an infant in a stroller had stopped to ask.

"They've found the truck, and they think they know the identity of that Shortcut Stalker."

"That guy who took all the little girls?"

"Yeah." The salesman leaned against the end of a display counter. "That asshole is as good as dead. He better hope he doesn't get thrown in with the general population, 'cause he won't never make it to the gas chamber if that happens."

"If you ask me," The Monster said, "The parents are just as much to blame as that man they're looking for."

A groan of protest went up. Everybody started talking at once, but he was bigger and louder. "What were those girls doing out after dark – alone?"

A commercial break gave some an excuse to wander away. None of the remaining shoppers had any interest in arguing with this big, angry man.

"Sure. There are always going to be men out there who can't control themselves, but there would be no victims if the parents would supervise their kids properly. You ask me, parents like that don't deserve to have little girls in the first place."

In the silence that followed his angry outburst, Jack had looked beyond the glass doors to see his taxi pull up to the curb. He strode away confidently, leaving behind a group of uneasy shoppers to exchange looks and shake their heads.

"What an asshole." The salesman had been overheard to say.

21. OH! *THAT* LIGHT!

Charity hovered over them. Her father's vulnerability had been devastating to watch. The lone tear that had escaped his eye the night of her abduction had been the closest she had ever come to witnessing a breach in his defenses. He had always been unstoppable, unbreakable. But, here he was, broken, sobbing and childlike in her mother's embrace. It had all been too much for him. Seeing every stranger as suspect. Staying on top of the FBI's every move, and making certain that Charity's case had remained an active investigation – though nothing had been found week after agonizing week. Every time the phone rang it had made him jump.

Now, to get this news – news he had been waiting and hoping and praying for – so suddenly and unexpectedly -- had caused the tides of emotion to wash over all of his carefully-constructed barricades. The world was watching, and he knew it. The time for fortitude had come and he had crumbled.

Yet, how beautiful her mother had been in that moment! She had radiated strength and compassion. Her back had been straight and her arms had become a fortress within which he could find refuge. A startling ferocity had transformed her features to those of a warrior queen, and had infused her russet eyes with a luminosity that was transcendent.

Charity felt herself being filled to the top of her head with light. Rays of it burst from her fingertips and from the ends of her hair. She had never experienced anything so powerful before.

Except for the night I spoke to Billy. The night I was murdered.

With every ounce of hope she could muster, Charity dropped to the earth in front of her parents.

"Mom? Can you see me? Can you hear me?"

When her mother had looked up and met her eyes for the first time since that horrible night, Charity knew that she was getting through. The light that had filled both of them was the way. Charity's heart burst with the knowledge and understanding that had been eluding her.

"Mama."

Her mother nodded. Tears in her eyes; the light still shining through her with blinding radiance.

"I love you so much, Mama. I'm so proud of you."

"My baby girl, how I've missed you."

"I know Mama. I've been with you all along. This is the man's truck. He is the one who hurt me." Charity lifted her hand to point at the dark remains of Jack's Ford. "But, Billy was telling you the truth. I'm really okay. I can hardly even remember what that man did to me. It seems like a very long time ago."

The tears flowed freely from her mother's eyes, and she had bent to whisper something to Charity's dad.

"Our baby is here, Dan. Look behind you. She is here, and I can see her. I can hear her, honey. I can hear her. She is okay. Look."

Her dad was hesitant to raise his tear-stained face from the shelter of his wife's shoulder, but he did, and he looked behind him, but he didn't have the light and he couldn't see.

"Daddy can't see me." Charity said, gently. "It is the light. You are filled with the light."

Her mother nodded, somehow understanding.

"Mama, my body. . ." Charity paused and looked away. "It doesn't exist anymore. He destroyed it."

Another nod; her mother seemed at peace.

"I don't know how much longer I'll be allowed to stay here. Sometimes, I feel. . . as though there is someplace else I need to go. . ."

"We will be strong, now. I promise that we will be strong." Her mother's words had seemed to be directed at her father, and he had nodded his agreement.

"Yes. We are strong. Together, we are." He began to dry his face and try to pull himself together. Her parents had kissed and embraced, and in a final blinding burst of radiance, Charity had waved goodbye for the last time.

ABOUT THE AUTHOR

Kaye Marie Giuliani was born in Washington, DC in 1959. She was raised in Maryland and still resides there with her husband (and childhood sweetheart) Gilbert Giuliani, Jr.